This book is dedicated to my daughter, Cara Pelletier,
who edited this book
and to my granddaughter, Beatrix Pelletier Gregoire,
who test read it for me.

Written by Linda D Vincent

Illustrations by Pavani Apsara

For inquiries, please contact: Linda Vincent linda@lindadvincent.com

ISBN: 978-1-7381136-0-6

Printed in Canada

Emma's Day at the Seaside Cottage

Written by Linda D Vincent
and
Illustrated by Pavani Aspara

Emma woke up slowly. There was a soft breeze coming in through her window and just a bit of daylight filtering through the curtains. Then she remembered "We're at the cottage!" and a wave of excitement came over her.

The cottage was quiet so Emma knew that Mommy and Daddy were still asleep. She tip-toed through the living room and out to the front porch so as not to wake them up.

It was beautiful outside! There was a bit of fog in the air but it was slowly burning off in the sunshine. The wooden porch was as wide as the cottage and Emma leaned over the railing, soaking in the sights of a maritime morning. There was a bit of grass in front of the cottage. It was damp with dew sparkling in the sunlight. Beyond the grass was a sandy beach leading down to beautiful blue water with little waves lapping at the shore. Emma knew that her parents wouldn't want her to go any further. In fact, they wouldn't want her to be out at all while they were still asleep. She stayed on the front porch breathing in the salt air and listening to the early morning sounds of seagulls flying above. She sank down onto a chair, feeling really good about being on vacation here.

Before too long, she started to hear sounds of movement inside the cottage. Daddy stepped outside the door to enjoy the seaside view too. "There you are," he said. "I was worried when I didn't see you in your bed." "If you wake up before we do, don't go any further than the porch," he said. "I know that, Daddy," Emma said as she got out of the chair and gave him a big good-morning hug.

They had driven through lots of small towns to get to the seaside cottage. She wanted to see what this one was like. Emma went inside to her room and quickly got dressed.

In the kitchen, Mommy had a simple breakfast ready for Emma. It had to be simple because they only brought a few things with them. Later, when they brought groceries back from town, there would be a lot more. This morning Emma had orange juice, toast with peanut butter, and a large glass of milk. She liked toast with peanut butter so that was just fine with her.

While Mommy and Daddy were washing up and getting ready to go into town, Emma went to the cozy living room and looked through the books in the bookcase. They were all big people books so they looked pretty boring to her. She couldn't find any that she wanted to read. Emma sighed. She wished there were books she could read.

The drive to town was along a country road with lots of trees and just a few homes here and there. When they came into town, they found the grocery store near the end of the main street, the longest street in town. There were stores all along it. They drove past a library, clothing stores, souvenir shops, restaurants, and the town hall.

After parking the car, Daddy went into the grocery store to get food for their stay at the cottage.

Mommy and Emma took a walk and looked into some shops while Daddy was shopping. The third store was a book store! Emma had already told Mommy that there were no children's books at the cottage. They went into the store and started looking at all the books. Emma found a book she wanted. It was about the adventures of a princess. Mommy found a children's book about sea shells. "Would you like this book, Emma?" she asked. It had pictures of different kinds of shells so Emma would know what they were when she found them on the beach. Emma liked that book too, so Mommy bought both.

By now Daddy had finished the grocery shopping and was putting the food into the car. "Come on, ladies," he said. "We've got to get back and have lunch so we can go swimming this afternoon."

After lunch at the cottage, it was "quiet time." Mommy said "We can't go into the water until one hour after eating," so it was time to rest or read. Emma wasn't tired so she decided to look at her sea shells book. Daddy checked for messages on his cell phone, while Mommy found a book that looked interesting and started reading that.

Finally quiet time ended. Emma scrambled to get her bathing suit on, while Mommy and Daddy changed into theirs in their room.

Emma had brought some sand toys with her: a pail, a shovel, and some sand molds. Mommy brought beach towels for them. They excitedly headed for a nice spot on the beach, close to the water. Mommy laid out the towels for them. Daddy had the water bottles and sunscreen. "Can we go in the water now"? Emma asked. "Yes, Emma, we can go in the water. Don't go too deep and stay in this area near to us," Mommy said. "I think I'll come too," she added.

Mommy and Emma slipped off their sandals and slowly waded into the water. It was cold at first but Emma didn't care. She knew it would feel warmer after she got further in.

In fun, Emma reached down, scooped some water up, and splashed Mommy. Mommy shrieked but then she splashed Emma back.

It felt cold so Emma ducked under so the water was all the way up to her shoulders. That felt cold too but just for a moment and then Emma started to warm up. Emma walked along, kneeling to keep her shoulders under the water. She pushed her arms back to move herself forward, as if she was swimming. This was fun! She could sit on the bottom and still keep her head above water. The water was cloudy where the sand had been stirred up but it cleared when she sat still. Emma could see the sand and pebbles at the bottom. She looked for sea shells but she couldn't see any.

Later when Mommy and Emma came out of the water, Emma found a good place to sit in the sand, where she could dig and search for shells. Mommy sat on a beach towel and watched Emma play. Now that they were back on shore, Daddy decided it was his turn to go for a swim. Daddy was a strong swimmer and could swim a good distance but he stayed in an area of water that was roped off for safety.

Emma took her sand pail and scooped a bucket full of water, then dumped it where she wanted to dig in the sand. She dug and she filled her pail with wet sand and then dumped it out to form a small tower. She did this over and over until she had a row of sand towers and a good-sized hole in the sand.

Finally, when she thought there was nothing in the hole except pebbles and sand, she saw the edge of something different. She eagerly dug and pulled it out. It was a clam shell! Emma was very excited to have found a shell. She showed Mommy right away. Emma was right. It was a clam shell!

After that, other children who were playing on the beach came over and asked if they could dig with her too. They turned out to be a sister and brother named Melissa and Jared. They all had fun together, digging in the sand, making sand towers, and looking for shells. Jared found a clam shell too, but they couldn't find any more.

By now, Emma and her family had been out in the sun long enough. No one wanted to get a sunburn, so they gathered up their things and headed back to the cottage. Emma would have liked to stay longer but she knew they would have lots of time at the beach during the rest of their vacation.

There was a gas barbeque on concrete in front of the cottage, just before where the grass started. There was a fire pit further out in the middle of the grass lawn. It had large stones around it and sand between the stones and the place where the logs burned. "Can we have a camp fire tonight?" Emma asked. "A little later after dinner," Daddy said. "Just play outside in the shade here until dinner is ready. We're going to do hamburgers on the BBQ."

Emma was very hungry after the fresh air and activity of the afternoon. She ate a big hamburger, lots of potato chips, and a little bit of salad. She finished off with a bowl of raspberries on ice cream, a chocolate chip cookie, and a tall glass of milk. She was stuffed!

Daddy pulled three lawn chairs out and set them around the camp fire. Emma climbed into one of them and watched Daddy build the fire. He started with some crumpled paper, added twigs, then put big logs on top. Daddy had been a Scout when he was a boy, so he knew how to make a camp fire! He lit the crumpled paper and it started to burn, spreading upwards to the larger logs. Pretty soon he had a roaring camp fire going.

He and Mommy sat down with their tea, to enjoy the fire. Emma couldn't eat or drink another thing!

As the sun was setting, she curled up in the chair and enjoyed the crackling of the fire and the dancing of the flames. She could hear the sea lapping softly at the shore. It was hypnotic and soon Emma was feeling very sleepy.

As she thought about their first day at the seaside, she remembered the beautiful, slightly foggy morning view that she had awakened to. She thought about the trip to town and the books she bought. She remembered with pleasure swimming in the ocean, digging in the sand, finding a clam shell, and making friends with Melissa and Jared.

She could hear the sounds of Mommy and Daddy's voices as they talked together nearby and she felt very safe and secure.

"Thank you, God," she said quietly in her head, "for a nice day and for this beautiful world that you made."

With that, Emma was gone to dreamland. She was so sound asleep that she didn't even feel Daddy lifting her up and carrying her to her bed. Tomorrow would be another day with new adventures!

The End

Manufactured by Amazon.ca
Acheson, AB